Joe Bright and the
Seven Genre Dudes

Jackie Mims Hopkins
Illustrations by John Manders

Janesville, Wisconsin
www.upstartbooks.com

For Leanne Drake, my library partner and
story tella extraordinaire.
—J. M. H.

To Lisa
—J. M.

Published by UpstartBooks
401 S. Wright Road
Janesville, WI 53547-1368
1-800-448-4887

Text © 2010 by Jackie Mims Hopkins
Illustrations © 2010 by John Manders

The paper used in this publication meets the minimum requirements
of American National Standard for Information Science — Permanence
of Paper for Printed Library Material. ANSI/NISO Z39.48.

Far, far away in a storybook kingdom, there lived a master storyteller named Stella. The stories she told cast spells of enchantment upon all who listened. Stella took great pride in her storytelling abilities.

Each day Stella consulted her magic storybook which was carved in a grand wooden chair. She asked,

> "Storybook, storybook, carved upon the chair,
> who is the storyteller extraordinaire?"

And the book always replied,

> "You, Stella, are a great story tella!"

Satisfied, Stella would sit and read in the chair, knowing that the storybook always spoke the truth.

But one day when Stella asked the magic storybook her favorite question, it answered,

"You, Stella, are talented it's true,
but Joe Bright is quite a storyteller, too."

"Joe Bright! Who is Joe Bright? Show me this fella, this so-called story tella!" demanded Stella.

Stella watched angrily as the storybook revealed Joe Bright entertaining hundreds of listeners with his engaging tales.

"He must be stopped immediately!" shrieked Stella. And with that, she hatched a plan.

Stella gave her pet raven, Edgar, a bogus storytelling festival invitation.

"Hand this invitation to Joe and lead him deep into the dark forest so he is never seen or heard from again," she instructed.

Faithful Edgar took the invitation to Joe and escorted him into the dense forest.

When they were miles into the woods, Edgar suddenly flew away, leaving poor Joe confused and alone.

After wandering for several hours, Joe stumbled upon a house that he thought might be the festival headquarters.

He went inside and found a long dining table with seven place settings and seven chairs. On the other side of the room there were seven beds an seven bookcases. Exhausted, Joe plopped himself down on one of the bed and fell fast asleep.

Soon, the seven brothers who lived in the house came home from work and found Joe snoring away. Gathering around him they all shouted, "Wake up!"

A startled Joe fell out of the bed and asked, "Are you guys my audience?"

"No, we live in this house," they chorused. "Who are you and what are you doing here?"

"My name is Joe Bright, and I am a storyteller. I thought your house might be the storytelling festival headquarters, so I let myself in."

"Ohhh, we've heard of you and your legendary storytelling," said the brothers. "We work at the Friends of the Forest Library where we're known as The Seven Genre Dudes. Each of us is in charge of certain genres or kinds of literature at the library. Allow us to introduce ourselves."

"I'm Nathaniel, and I take care of the nonfiction. Books about real people, places, and things are my responsibility."

"Hello, I'm Reggie, and I'm in charge of the realistic fiction books. My stories have made-up characters and events, but they seem very real."

"My name is Sherlock, and I manage the mysteries. My books will keep you on the edge of your seat with characters who try to solve crimes or unexplained events."

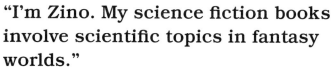

"I'm Zino. My science fiction books involve scientific topics in fantasy worlds."

"Hi, I'm Henry, and I look after the historical fiction. My stories are set in historical times."

"My name is Jack, and I watch over several kinds of books in the folk literature genre. You'll find magic, talking animals, and make-believe worlds when you read my fairy tales, folktales, myths, fables, and legends."

"Last, but not least, I'm Hink Pink, and I tend to the poetry. My books have rhythm and rhyme."

"The library is in need of a storyteller," said Sherlock. "Would you be interested in the job, Joe?"

"I would love it!" replied Joe.

The next morning, Joe and The Seven Genre Dudes went to the library. Storytime with Joe was a big hit. Children, animals, and adults came from far and near to hear Joe's magical stories.

Now Stella, believing that Joe was lost in the woods forevermore, went to her magic storybook and said,

"Storybook, storybook, carved upon the chair,
who is the storyteller extraordinaire?"

And the book answered,

"You, Stella, are talented it's true,
but Joe Bright at the library
is quite a storyteller, too."

"Joe is telling stories at the library?" Stella cried. "I must put an end to that at once!"

Stella thought and thought about how she could stop Joe Bright. Finally, she arrived at the perfect solution.

"I know!" she said. "I'll take away his storytelling memory. He will be unable to remember a word, and I will be the best storyteller once again."

Stella baked a batch of scrumptious cupcakes with a memory-erasing cream filling. The next afternoon, she disguised herself as a baker and went to the library. Joe was outside under a tree enjoying the last of his lunch when Stella arrived.

"I have baked special cupcakes just for you, Joe," she said sweetly.

"Just in time for dessert! Thank you," said Joe, gobbling up a treacherous treat.

When Joe went into the library to begin his afternoon storytime, he felt a bit peculiar.

"Once upon a . . ." he began.

"Once upon . . ."

"What's happening?" cried Joe. "I can't remember my story!"

"Don't worry," said Sherlock, "We'll help you."

And one by one, the Genre Dudes told Joe stories.

Sherlock told him several mysteries. Joe's favorite was *The Case of the Creaking Bones.*

Henry's stories were historical fiction. One was about a soldier in the Civil War, and another was set in ancient Rome.

Jack's folk literature tales were next. There were stories of Paul Bunyan, Snow White, gods and goddesses, and Aesop's fables.

Reggie told a realistic fiction story about a family moving to a new town and another about a girl and her dog.

Joe listened to Nathaniel's nonfiction biographies of Abraham Lincoln and Christopher Columbus.

Hink Pink entertained Joe with poems. Some of the poems rhymed, some were silly, and others had a serious tone.

One of Zino's science fiction stories was about a robot named X.E.5, who lived in a world where humans were the enemy.

When the Genre Dudes were finished telling their stories, Joe had many stories to tell!

The next day, a messenger in a royal coach arrived at the library and read an invitation from the king.

"You are hereby invited to perform before his majesty and the royal court this evening at six o'clock."

"Please tell the king I would be honored to perform for him," said Joe.

rly that evening, when Stella checked in with her beloved magic storybook, she ard some distressing news.

"You, Stella, are talented it's true,
but Joe Bright, in the king's court,
is quite a storyteller, too."

aaaugh!" screamed Stella. "*I* should be in the king's court telling stories, not e Bright! There's only one thing left to do. I must take away his voice! After all, at good is a storyteller without a voice?" she cackled.

ella went to her secret potion room where she created a silencing solution for e's drinking water.

When Stella arrived at the castle, Joe had already begun his story. She clutched her potion bottle and tried not to listen to his enticing voice, but she was drawn in like a butterfly to nectar. When Joe's story ended, the crowd cheered and Stella stood in awe. After taking his bow, Joe looked up and pointed to Stella.

"Is your name Stella?" he asked.

"Why, yes, it is," she answered. "How did you know my name?"

"For many years, I have admired your wonderful storytelling. I've always dreamed of becoming a master storyteller just like you, and now, here we are together in the king's royal court!"

The king beamed at Stella and Joe and said, "Stella, I already knew of your remarkable talent, but I wanted to know if Joe was good enough to work with you. That is why I invited him here today. Both of you have a powerful gift that should be shared with everyone. The two of you shall travel throughout my kingdom spreading the joy of stories. And each week, you shall return to the Friends of the Forest Library, where you will entertain us all with tales of your journeys."

So Stella and Joe, a pair extraordinaire, rolled away in a royal coach, and told stories happily forever after.